For all the animals,
human or otherwise,
we've met in Asia
—C.F. & E.R.

Text copyright © 2012 by Candace Fleming
Illustrations copyright © 2012
by Eric Rohmann

Published in the United States by
Schwartz & Wade Books, an imprint of
Random House Children's Books,
a division of Random House, Inc., New York.
Schwartz & Wade Books and the colophon
are trademarks of Random House, Inc.
Visit us on the Web! randomhouse.com/kids
Educators and librarians, for a variety
of teaching tools, visit us at
randomhouse.com/teachers
Library of Congress
Cataloging-in-Publication Data
Fleming, Candace.
Oh, no! / Candace Fleming; [illustrations by
Eric Rohmann].
—1st ed.
p. cm.
Summary: A series of animals falls into a
deep hole, only to be saved at last by a
very large rescuer.
ISBN 978-0-375-84271-9 (trade)
ISBN 978-0-375-94557-1 (glb)
[1. Stories in rhyme. 2. Animals—Fiction.]
I. Rohmann, Eric, ill. II. Title.
PZ8.3.F63775Oh 2011   [E]—dc22
2009045564
The text of this book is set in Archetype.
The illustrations are relief prints made using
the reduction method.
MANUFACTURED IN CHINA
10 9 8 7 6 5 4 3 2 1
First Edition

Oh, No!

Words by
CANDACE FLEMING

Pictures by
ERIC ROHMANN

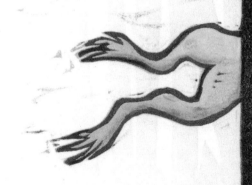

schwartz & wade books · new york

Frog fell into a deep, deep hole.

Ribbit-oops!

Ribbit-oops!

Frog fell into a deep, deep hole.

Ribbit-oops!

Frog fell into such a deep hole,

he couldn't get out to save his soul.

Croaked Frog, "Help! Help! I can't get out!"

Mouse came along, but what could she do?

Pippa-eeek!

Pippa-eeek!

Mouse came to help, but what could she do?

Pippa-eeek!

Mouse was so small, what could she do?

She tried reaching down,

and she fell in, too.

Squeaked Mouse, "We're trapped!

We can't get out!"

Loris inched down from her banyan tree.

Soo-slooow!

Soo-slooow!

Loris inched down from her banyan tree.

Soo-slooow!

Loris inched down

from that high-up tree.

Then her allergy

to cats made her—

ACHOO!

—sneeze.

Sniffled Loris,

"Bless me!

We can't get out."

Sun Bear lowered a whopping big branch.

Grab on!

Grab on!

Sun Bear lowered a whopping big branch.

Grab on!

Sun Bear lowered that big, big branch.

But with the weight of all those critters,

he teetered . . .

tottered . . .

CRASHED!

Grumbled Sun Bear,

"Bad luck! We can't get out!"

Monkey swung by
on his kudzu vine.

Wheee-haaaa!

Wheee-haaaa!

Monkey swung by
on his kudzu vine.

Wheee-haaaa!

He was having such
fun on his kudzu vine,
he didn't see
that tree in time.

Groaned Monkey,
"Ouch! Ow!
We can't get out!"
Oh, no!

Now Tiger slunk over and licked his teeth.

Slop-slurp!

Slop-slurp!

Tiger slunk over and licked his teeth.

Slop-slurp!

Tiger narrowed his eyes and licked his teeth.

He smiled at the sight of his tasty feast.

Drawled Tiger, "I'm here to help you out."

Oh, no!

Then the ground bumble-rumbled and began to shake.

BA-BOOM!

BA-BOOM!

The ground bumble-rumbled and began to quake.

BA-BOOM!

The ground bumble-rumbled and quake-shake-quaked.

And look who came to help them escape. . . .

Hooray!

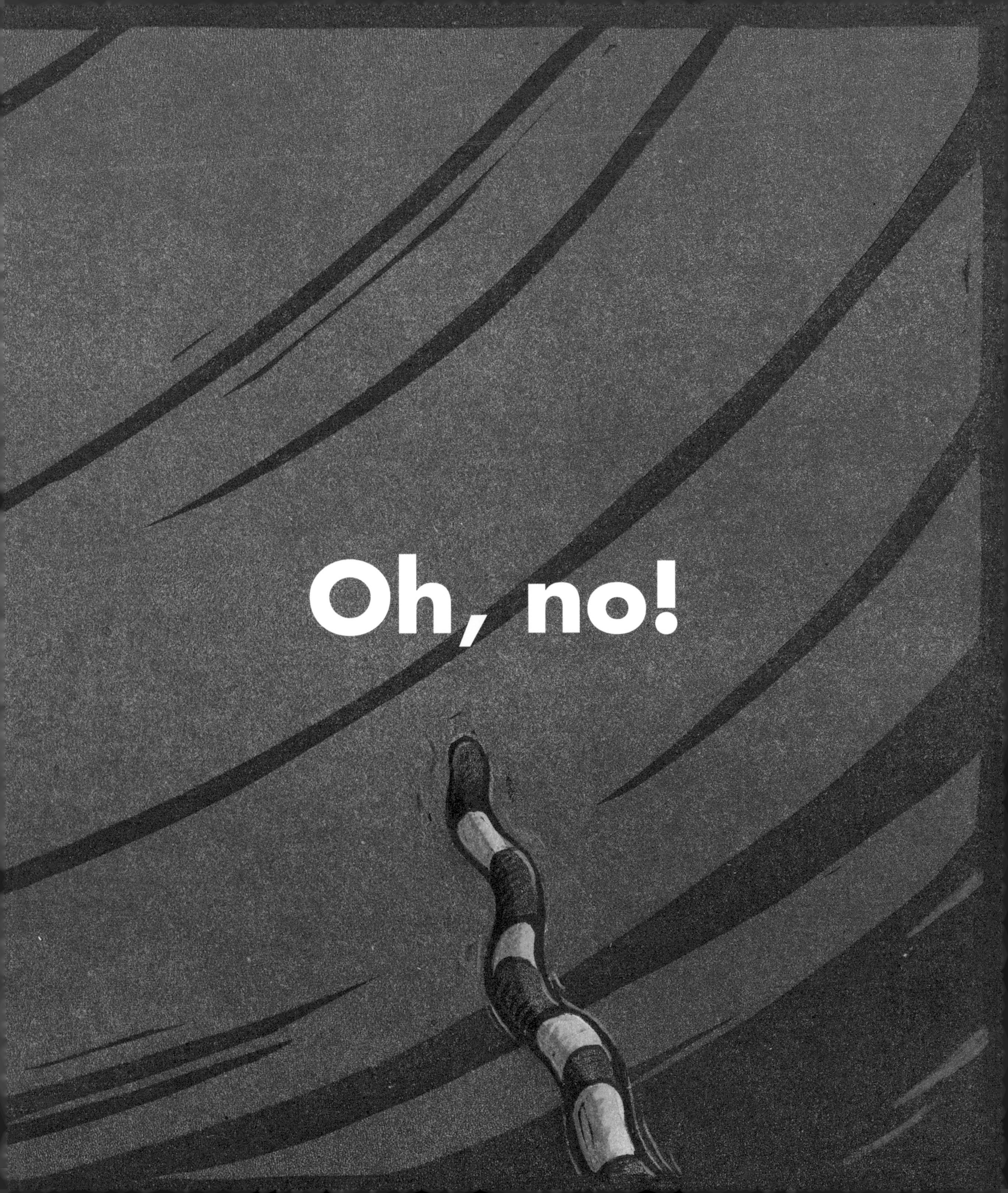

Oh, no!

Tiger fell into the deep, deep hole.

Grrr-owwwl!

Grrr-owwwl!

Tiger fell into the deep, deep hole.

Grrr-owwwl!

Tiger fell into
such a deep hole,

he couldn't jump out
to save his soul.

Wailed Tiger, "Please, please,
won't you help me out?"